I0542579

Relentless
REALITIES
A Collection
Of Poems

ROY MERCHANT

Relentless Realities

Dedication

To my wife, my children, my family
And all the friends
Who collectively nourishes me.

Thank you.

Acknowledgements

I Would like to thank the editor who worked on this tirelessly for me to get it out error-free. Towards the end of the writing, I could not see a missing comma, full stop, or hyphen if it came up and slapped me in the face. Thanks to Christopher Walker for the work he did in helping to turn these ideas from lumps of stones to something I am very proud of.

A great big thank you to my reading group who sat through my readings and gave me insights and inspirational thoughts when I needed them.

Contents

Preface

I never intended to publish my poems. I wrote them down because they came to me as thoughts on a wave and demanded to be noticed by me, but never to be published.

I just kept writing them down, and I shared a few with my wife, my brothers and sisters, and very close friends. I even read a few at events over the years, but they were never to be shared with the world.

Then a few years back, I began a long journey of illness and out of that came my first published book Walking in the Shadows of Death, a book of poetry and prose charting my journey from hope to hopelessness and back again. Numerous people who read the book encouraged me to publish my completed poems, hence this book.

I say the words come to me as thoughts on a wave. If that is difficult to imagine, then another way to describe it is to say that sometimes it feels like I live near a pool, and in that pool are all the words to describe anything and everything.

The pool is not a real pool, you understand, it is a pool of my heart, my soul, my imagination. I go to that pool sometimes when I am happy, sad, reflective, ecstatic or just plain emotionally neutral. Invariably, I come away with a piece of poetry or prose that reflects my mood.

You could say that I should go to the pool every day and bring something back, but that would not be a good use of my intuition as my feelings tell me when to go to the pool, and I am in there right now.

Over time, the pool has given me insight into different thoughts, feelings and differing points of view. Different worlds, in fact. These are what I want to share with you in this collection.

Introduction

My name is Roy Merchant, and I am from Jamaica, an island of close to three million inhabitants in the Caribbean Sea.

I have lived in the United Kingdom since 1961 and whilst I have had many professions in my seventy-one years on planet Earth, from a submariner in the Royal Navy in my early years, an electronics engineer in my middle years and finishing as a local government manager at the end, I have always been passionate about writing.

I remember writing a poem at the age of six, which I recited in the main Seventh-day Adventist Church of Jamaica in Kingston at the age of seven.

I lost the passion in the early years of my life in England. The pain of adjustment to the English way of life eroded the desire. It was only in the early '70s when I left the Navy and began to make some sense of where I was and who I was becoming, that I began to reconnect with the 'Creative Pool' again.

The 'Pool' for me is a place where I go fishing for words. Sometimes they instantly make perfect sense; sentences, or phrases to which my thoughts can give meaning. Other times, they just hang there for months until clarity fights its way through the mist and comes to me.

I have published two books, the first entitled *Walking in the Shadows of Death*, which looks at the battle between hope and hopelessness and how I came to terms with the new me after my near-death journeys.

The latest is *called 20 Things I Wish I knew At 20*, which is self-explanatory. They are both available on Amazon for download and in paperback.

This collection is divided into two parts.

Part One is entitled Relentless Realities (I Have These Thoughts Sometimes) and encapsulates my shorter poems.

This section is arranged into seven sections; these subdivisions reflect some themes I would like to share with the reader. I think of them as more like songs and cries as opposed to simple compositions. The sections are:

My First Collection:	Songs for the Rich Dark Brown Shade of My Skin
	These are songs or poems that reflect the soul and mind-searching that goes on as a black man in a land where you are part of a minority, especially when your voice finds it difficult to be heard. After a while, you become uncertain why things never seem to end up how you thought they should, and you wonder what is going to happen next.

My Second Collection:	Songs So Small and Lucid

These are tiny poems, which say it all in a very tiny space. The collection is about the observation of wonderment and thoughts that fill us with perplexity and awe.

My Third Collection: Songs of Praise and Thanksgiving
This selection of poems is about the awesomeness and power of faith, hope and belief.

My Fourth Collection: Songs of Insight and Wisdom
These poems reflect insight on certain topics I have gained along the way. They mostly capture the frailties we human beings hide, protect and endure on our way from the birth canal to the death canal.

My Fifth Collection: Songs of Love and Longing
These verses are about the power of love, the absence of love, the pain of love, and the humour of love. They look at all love: the love of family, sibling love, doomed love, hopeful love, naïve love, and the uncertainty of it all.

My Sixth Collection: Songs for the Silver Years
I have two compositions in this section, as I did not wish to dwell here too long. This is the only inescapable part of life if you

want to keep living. Best to take it in your stride, with a positive outlook and a strident gait. There Is No Pain reminds me that there are painful Octobers when the sun no longer shines and the four horsemen remember my name.

My Seventh Collection: Songs of Reflection
This collection is a montage of different thoughts. From the sad, devastated The Traveller, to No More Tears from Baghdad, Communication to the final beauty of My Words, My Lines.

Part two   The Long Songs Collection
This collection entitled The Long Songs and encapsulates my longer poems. The Long Songs are my epic poems of death, the battle between hope and hopelessness, illness, history, and finally the resilience of man through the use of hope.

PART ONE

I have these thoughts sometimes

SONGS FOR THE RICH DARK BROWN SHADE OF MY SKIN

These poems were written over a period where I became aware that the colour of my skin would/could have a profound effect on the life I was going to lead.

In Jamaica, we were never aware of prejudice and discrimination. If someone didn't like you, they had a tangible reason for that. Maybe you disrespected his daughter or his wife or kicked his mule when you thought he wasn't looking. It would have been something that after a conversation or even a fight you could do something about. That sense of "I can resolve it once I know about it" was a cornerstone in the mindset of the people in our village, our town, our country. Then we came to England.

In England, people would discriminate against you because of the colour of your skin, which meant you had unresolvable problems because you could not change the colour of your skin (some tried, believe me, some tried) and the hate could not be assuaged. There was nothing you could do about it. Nothing at all.

You became increasingly aware of the phenomenon at school, at work, in the Navy-everywhere. It permeated every action and every reaction you made in the environment in which you found yourself. And you wondered whether the decision that a white person took was based on the colour of your skin? Or the action you took? You just did not know.

In time, you wondered if any friendship between you and your white colleagues was real. Was the smile genuine or just a parting of the lips to hide the real feelings?

Some of us were crushed by discrimination and prejudice. Some of us withstood the pressure and became diamonds. Sometimes, though, it is difficult to work out who is who. This section is dedicated to us all.

Eyeless in Babylon

I went to work one morning,
The man said I work too slow,
But as I looked around me,
No one else was on the go.

He calls me in his office,
Questioning my attitude,
And as I look around me
Five others were being rude.

Now, I am quite sensible,
I know I'm not paranoid,
But between me and the others
There is a great big void.

We went to a club one evening,
Four other friends and I,
The music and drinks were good,
My friend, I tell no lie.

So, we're coming out the club
Feeling so drunk and high,
I was the only one to be picked up,
My friends, I wonder why.

I'm beginning to see a difference
Between me and the rest,
I always end up on the floor,
I never come off best.

The pressure is being applied,
To make me a second-class man.
At last, I'm beginning to see it,
I wonder why it all began.

The pressure is so subtle,
A spider's web is spun.
And how can you win this battle?
When you're eyeless in Babylon.

Oh, I don't know if it's important,
And I'm probably way off track,
But the colour of my skin,
Just happens to be black.

Matter of Opinion

I was walking down to town
My pocket empty...but a pound
Mind just going round and round
Depression occupying my inner ground
Needed to erase the labyrinth-like frown
By listening to some loud, loud sound

Let the music fulfil my wish
Separate the mash from the mish
Allow my hopelessness to vanish
Positive attitude to replenish
Must relieve my hunger with a dish
Spent ten pence on an out-of-date fish

Met an old lady...borrowed some scallion
When I met upon this interesting opinion

The opinion's attitude was small
And I was quite honestly appalled
At how a man who stood so tall
Ends up seeing nothing at all
So, I put my fish down on the wall
And listened to the opinion who came to call

6 ☾ Roy Merchant

The opinion said...
It can't excuse the blacks
For the confidence, they lack
On the way, they're hanging back
And seem to be way off track
Killing themselves with coke and crack

No workable schemes
Just futile themes
No economical teams
Just implausible dreams
No controlled means
Just watery streams.

I looked at the opinion with sad, sad eyes
And thought to myself ... when will... you realise?
Why can't you have the insight to surmise?
That the last four centuries are based on lies
It wasn't a question of you being overly wise
Your technology was too strong ... and you heard no cries

How can you know the feeling?
When the rejections send you reeling
When you can't see ... with what you're dealing
When it's 1963 ... and you're living in Ealing

If you really understood my history
You would see that there's no mystery
No misconstruing of my reality
I have looked and looked, but I cannot see
The things you think you see in me

What I have is your portion of life's misery
That you have force-fed me
So that you can be

I may be a little insecure
But at least I am no sinecure
It may be that I'm not pure
It may be that I'm not sure
It may be that the way ahead is obscure
But my spirit is strong … the pain I'll endure

So …
You have your day, and I'll have mine
Today is your day, enjoy the wine
But … as sure as night follows day
Tomorrow is mine

He went on his way no wiser a man
I smiled the smile of one who can understand
You can only prevent it if you recognise the plan
I picked up my fish, and two pieces of scallion
Sat on the pavement, listened to the band
Feeling so good, I embraced the land.

We Gonna Build the Nation

We are going to build a nation
Built out of wisdom and elation
It will have a rock-solid foundation
Based on love and education
We're going to build a civilisation
Which moves us on from emancipation
Which merges our history and imagination
To create a world of unification

We will teach our children the value of simply giving
The joy to be got from simple living
Our nation will be a peaceful place
Open to all members of the human race

We will have to forget the sins of the past
No point dwelling on wickedness so vast
We must be imaginative and act really fast
To create something that is going to last.

We have to do it now; we have to make a start
We have to be engaged; we have to play our part.
If we wait for others to do it, we might as well depart
Let us find the courage to do it, let us find the heart.

When we finish, we can look back and smile
Original man, we have been here a while
Out of Africa, we have travelled a million miles
All of man's experience is stored in our files
Forgiveness is our primary weapon, so let's bury the bile
And move forward on the journey in a confident style

So...my friend, you can have your day, and I'll have mine
Today is your day, enjoy the wine
But ... just remember, yesterday was and tomorrow is ... mine.

Packit Eena Mi Han

Ah was standin on de Kahna
Packit eena mi han
Lef fut in front a de adda
Tinkin I look gran

Ah was standing on de kahna
Shues palish till it staht to gleam
Tootpick eena de kahna mi mout
Tinking I was de Jemaacan dream

Standin on de kahna
Head held up high so deh kyann se di pain
Langin to be in Jemaaca
Jus fe get out a dis dyam rain

Standin on de kahna
Crombie button … till e kyan button no more
Yeye a tun up a look eena de sky,
An me a wonda weh him have in store

Standin on de kahna
A doan have a jab since a cum to dis lan
A fed-up a anemployment
A fed-up a holing up mi han

Standin on de kahna
Random taughts jus rattlin in my brain
Lookin down Ridley Road mahket
An observin de capitalis game

Standin on de kahna
Mercedes slush jus a dutty up mi shues
Driva a tun roun anna look pon mi
As if im know I Doan pay no dues

I am standin' on de kahna
De snow jus a tun mi head white
De most pressin ting dats on my mind
Is weh mi gweanh sleep ti nite

Standin on de kahna
Kyann seem to prove to dem dat de're wrong
Every ting I do jus seem to confirm
What dey've be'n tinkin all along

Standin on de kahna
Nobody sees the dreams in my heart
All dem si is weh dem si
Deh doan see what tears me apart

Me still standin on dis kahna
An it's not because all my dreams have come true
Ah standin on de kahna
'Cause dere is nothing else for me to do.

Africanus

As the war rages,
And the outcome is unsure.
Rather than waiting for euthanasia,
Africanus hides his genes in Caucasia.
Or is it the other way round?

Jamaica A Go Go

Jamaica sits there patiently
Waiting for the sun to shine.
Sitting there in retrospect
And Jamaica will never be mine

Further down the historical line
It will have to find its Mojo
But right now, in the wilderness
Jamaica is just A Go Go

Nonetheless
Jamaica smiles in its enigmatic way
Confident in its quiet way
Still waiting for the rain to end
And the start of a brighter day.

Bye Bye Miss St Anns

You lie there in your hospital bed,
Leg broken when falling downstairs.
Heart also broken and in a state of shock,
Waiting for your transport to Bart's,
To try and repair that broken heart.

You are worried about your husband,
Who you married 55 years ago.
You wonder if the carers turned up,
Hope they had not forgotten their key,
To your home, where hubby lays,
Dying of Big C.

You came to England all those years ago,
From a little village,
In the Parish of St Anns, Jamaica.
You and your boyfriend were going to change the world,
The handsome swagger boy and his island girl.

"Englan is Englan, good and bad.
Too busy to plan, too proud to run.
Day followed day; night followed night.
Wake up one morning, eighty years old,

And half our dreams just never unfold.
Swagger boy, still a swagger,
Island girl still a smile,
As we dance to Johnny Ace singing,
Pledging my love.
We rub a lickle rub and remember the days,
When we were young and full of the sun's rays.

Now it is no longer about climbing Mount Everest,
It's just finding a good place fe si dung and rest.

Pickney dem pass round regularly,
We buy a double plat in a Manor Park Cemetery.
Time soon come a hope we go togedda,
Cause neider of us could stan de pain,
Of being separated …
Again".

Walk Good

Walk Good, my ageing, disillusioned father.
As you travel this foreign land.
Seeking a little solitude,
Trying to hide,
To stay invisible,
In a culture that cares little for your kind.
That knows not your name,
Your contribution,
Your input into the place,
They call England.
Walk Good.

Walk Good my innocent Son.
Still thinking it is easy out there.
Being hypnotised by the fear they have for you,
And too naïve to see how it will end.
Forgetting you are not in control.
Their fear will hurt you,
Opportunities will disappear,
You will be ostracised,
Hypnotised by the negative views.
And by twenty,
Unless you are strong,

Willed, Guided,
Your bright light will start to disappear,
To Fade.
Walk Good

Walk Good my proud family,
Who knows not about giving in.
Who will strive for a better tomorrow,
Whilst today laughs at your pain.
But …This day is just a day,
A Twinkle in the eye.
So,
We will sort out what needs to be done,
The wine is not ours to taste.
Our job is to prepare the land,
For what must come.
To prepare the mind,
For what must be.
The genes will be nourished and ready.
The DNA will be strong.
We will wait expectantly,
As we wave goodbye to the famine.
Walk Good.

Walk Good my patient people.
Been here all the time.
Ran the place for 10,000 years.
Paying the price for relaxing too soon,
Whilst others stole the prize.
I hope we are learning the lessons,
And will never be complacent again.

Been in the wilderness since 1492,
We gave them writing to taunt us with,
We gave them mathematics to fool us with,
We gave them gunpowder to kill us with,
And the sun shines on them right now.
But tomorrow will come.
Rome will fade.
Like China and India
We will come again.

Phoenixes do rise.
Civilisations come and go.
We evolve.
Our spirits stride the universes.
We will do it better next time.
Protecting humanity,
As best and for as long,
As ... we can.

It may not feel like it right now,
But in the depths of our despair,
We are probably at our best.
Walk Good.

1792

He calls me lazy and worthless,
Whilst sitting on the veranda all day,
Soaking in the gin.
He calls me nigger boy and treats my mother like dirt
It hurts, it hurts, it hurts like mad,
Because this nasty little man,
Is also, my biological dad.

My mother is beautiful.
So beautiful she cannot stay hidden
She tells me that's her curse.
The ugly girls only get beaten
What happens to her, is just so much worse

She smiles at him through frozen lips
Saying sweet nothings to avoid more physical pain
Her eyes, I have seen smile only twice
Once at me, the other to a man in Negril lane.

My father got up, paced the floor,
Shot me a box, smashed my head against the door.
Mum came running in from the molasses store,
Saw what was happening and couldn't take anymore.

Her spirit was freed and no longer afraid.
The future no longer hers to trade.
She grabbed the machete,
Whilst the crowd sensed the commotion.
Her final movements were poetry in motion.
This African warrior Queen.

Her first slash took off his head,
The eyes looked a little perplexed.
Head stayed in the air for a long, long time
Before knocking the gin bottle off the veranda.
Her second lunge was pointless,
It went for his heart,
But found,
Nothing there.

Imagined Realities?

Sister, Sister.
Broken down image of self.
Hates the indignity,
Hates the iniquity,
Hates the lip she bites till it bleeds.

Nothing to do but,
Sweep another floor.
Wipe another arse.
Smile another eye dead smile,
And belittle anyone who looks like her.

Brother, Brother.
Muscled till he kyaan muscle no more.
Hates the indignity,
Hates the iniquity,
Hates the lip he bites till it bleeds.

Nothing to do but,
Guard another shop.
Wash another car.
Push another trolley.
And thinks his master's house,
Is also…His.

SONGS SO SMALL
AND LUCID

I once heard a very bright and wise person suggest that the most significant concept can be articulated in less than twenty-five lines.

To do this, every word must be relevant, pointed and move the idea on to the next stage.

I hope I have achieved this in the following section.

Songs with many thoughts and ideas that are impossible to be contained within twenty-five lines are found in other sections of this collection.

The Watcher

She'd been all around the universe
She'd seen it in its prime
It seems as if she'd been watching it
Watching it all the time

She was born twenty trillion years ago
The only evolvement of its kind
She refused to dwell on the primitive myth called time
As it brought all those horrors to mind

In the backwaters of a far, far galaxy
In a solar system with a yellow sun
She first tested her great power
And created a thing she called ... man

She'd never been back to the experimental zone
Never bothered to see if her creation failed
She promised one day she would go and see
Whether the beings had even grown a tale!

The Kids at Fourteen

It seems just the other day
I was holding you in my arms
Holding you so close to me
Just to keep you warm

$$\underline{S}$$
$$\underline{I}$$
$$\underline{Z}$$
Now, look at the $\underline{E}$ of you.

Surprise

You bought a bed of indecision
Covered it …
With sheets of uncertainties
Slept on pillows …
With no definition
But you're still surprised
You have unfulfilled dreams.

Thoughts

Some people say they'd like to read minds
But I wonder if they have thought it through
I mean … how would you like to have some people
Imposing their thoughts on you?

Indecisiveness

Turning point ... oh, turning point,
Help me find the way.
Don't just sit there with your folded arms,
As I look for my needle in your hay.

Indecisive man ... oh, indecisive man
I've helped you all I can.
The answer is staring you in your face,
Just come up with the plan.

One Day with the Creams

Holding on to past dreams seems so easy
Holding ... and holding on is all it takes
Holding on to past dreams seems so easy
Until the idea is gone ... and you realise you're awake

I've been living in the promised land called tomorrow
I've been living in the promised land of my dreams
And in that land, there's no pain or no sorrow
Just a myriad ... of untried hopes and schemes

Take it all ... oh, take it all
Give me one proven move and take back all these dreams
Forsake it all ... I'll forsake it all
Just to put myself ... for one day with the creams

I'm forty-one years old ... and nothing's ever been easy
I'm forty-one years old ... and I've been climbing all the time
I need sometime ... to get over feeling weary
I need just one more day ... when I'm back at my prime

Holding on ... I'm holding on
Give me one proven move. And take back all these dreams.
Holding on. I'm holding on.
Just to put myself ... for one day with the creams.

Questions

How can you give spurious ... random directions?
While maintaining a myopic line
How do you cope with your desperation?
And pretend to the world you're fine
How do you shoot out your rapid-fire answers?
When ... only questions exist in your mind.

Shy Guy

I met this girl
Who had no curl
Her hair was straight and short
Her eyes so blue-ish
Her lips so small
And I loved her from the start.

It took me two years to say, "Hello."
Another year to say, "Hi."
It took her five seconds to say, "Who are you?"
And another two to say, "Goodbye."

A Slice of Time

You know I can't climb mountains
I know you have unfulfilled dreams
I know your love is like a fountain
At least, that's the way it seems.

My memories go back to December
When we made love for the very first time
Could it have been as I remember?
Was it really so sublime?

Now I'm feeling so lonely
Wishing you were here
You will be my only
Totally fulfilled affair.

Storming

Dissecting an original thought
And taking it too deep …
Can be like trying to analyse …
The random and abstract numbers…
In a bingo caller's basket …
Infinity will turn black to white.

As you get older
You seem to want more and more
Even when you don't know …
What you're looking for.
The master plan of our existence…
Just has to be a blank
The intricacies of persistence
That determines the totality.

I love … the feeling of insecurity
I love … just wanting to be free
I love … not knowing where I'll be
In 2023
I love … the fact that I can see
I love … the birds and the bees
But…I sometimes wonder if I love me.

Money and Power

Money, power and paranoia
Is a dangerous mixture
To have as a fixture
In a minuscule portion
Of the overall picture.

Lover's Contusion

The greatest contusion in a lover's life
Is the paradoxical confusion between
The circular movements of the mind
And the circular movements of the behind.

Looking Back

Sometimes
The only information ...
One gets from looking back
Is the realisation that ... you're way off track.
The only information I ever got
From peering at the past
Is the clarified certainty
Of the size of my task.

Life Is

Life Is Not Logical

Life Is Pure

Life Is Absolute

Whether You Are Pretty or Ugly,
Whether You Are Good, Weak or Strong,
Matters Not to Life.

It Owes You Nothing,

Not Even Your Next Breath.

Metallic Life

I'm sitting in this traffic jam
Observing the robot-like minds
And seeing how metallic life
Really screws up mankind.

Do they have a mind of their own?
Or ... are we in control?
They determine how fast we move
They don't always do as they're told.

If you were an alien
Looking down from afar
Who would you think the earthlings were?
The human ... or the car?

Inse/Sine...Cure

I was sitting there so insecure

She was sitting there so sinecure.

Spellbound

I've been looking at you looking at me
Shattering all your dreams

I've been looking at you looking at me
Screwing up all your schemes

I've been looking at you looking at me
Hurting you like hell

I've been looking at you looking at me
As if you're under a spell

I am looking at you looking at me
And I am trying to figure out why

I am looking at you looking at me
And there are no tears in your eye

You're looking at me looking at you
And it's always been the same

You looking at me looking at you
And I've always been wise…to your games.

The Twirling Pool

In the stillness of your inner mind
Where your secret thoughts are kept
Where all your truths are under lock and key
Even in those familiar places you've slept
There lies an idea in a twirling pool
Forever rotating its infinite tail
And hoping you'll return to it
When everything else has failed

The notion twists ... the notion bends
It's petrified of being ignored
It thinks it has the answers to life
That everyone is looking for

In the alien-like regions of your id
Where remnantic ... genetic memories do dwell
Where fractured schemes ... and sautéed dreams
Make up a world we call hell
There lies a man in a twirling pool
Forever rotating ... like a mindless snail
And praying ... something ... anything will rescue him
Before everything has failed

I met that man the other day
While I was making a cup of tea
As I stared down ... down into the murky depths
The man stared back at me.

Memories Of Medical Dissonance

I sat there remembering my simple disposition,
Glowing all around my confident countenance,
Now, hidden behind my fearful suppositions,
Created by overconfident medical dissonance.

SONGS OF PRAISE
AND THANKSGIVING

I was indoctrinated into the Seventh-day Adventist Church from a very early age and never questioned its doctrines, lessons, or ways while I was with my grandmother in the mountains of Jamaica.

It was the bright lights of London and my age, a questioning fourteen-year-old, which made me wonder whether there was any truth in the hefty tome—the cornerstone, the bedrock—that all the decisions my family ever made were based on. My challenging fourteen-year-old self quietly read the Bible from Genesis through to Revelations over a year, and then went straight back and reread it over six months. I decided that while it had grand narratives, amazing parables and moral ways to lead your life, there was no scientific basis for any of the stories.

I never really went back to it again until my younger children were born and I, in my forties, finally and reluctantly accepted the fact that there were powerful moral principles in the Bible that were worth passing on to the next generation.

At fifty, with the world at my feet and an ego-based success finally coming into view, I was struck down with an illness, which altered the course of my life. I could never go back to who I once was. In my search for, and ultimately understanding of, the new me, I turned to the Bible for insights. It did not let me down. I am eternally grateful for the Book of Job, which allowed me to bury the confidence of the uninformed that clothed me. Job made me realise that I was not in control and my ignorance was OK.

I have not fully accepted Yahweh, Jehovah, Jah or any other god. I do know, however, that there is a force much higher than I—and to that force, I give thanks and praises, awe and respect.
These songs are a small token of that gratitude.

Tell Me Sweet Lord (Job's Harvest)

Somewhere, out there, in a world so harsh
An ageing man wept a tear
He'd been working hard toiling the land
Solidly for a year.

There was nothing to show, nothing to see
For all the hard work he had done
The seeds were still lifeless in their pods
Like there was no rain or rising sun.

How would he feed his children?
What would the family do?
The ground just sat there looking lifeless
And hopelessness was all that grew.

On harvest morning, he sat in his fields
Quietly observing the land
Seeing barren fields where life should be
And trying to understand.

"My God, why hast thou forsaken me?
What have I done wrong?
Have I not been worshipping you?
Did you not hear my prayers and songs?

"You say you are the mighty one
You can do miracles in your sleep
You say you made the universe in six days
And yet, you just watch us weep.

"You said you would always be there for me
To protect me in times of strife
You know what was, what is and what will be

Yet you starve my children and wife.
"We cannot live a year without food
My family will surely die
Yet your power could have saved me
So, why? My Dear Lord, why?

"How could you fail to help me?
Why give me so much pain?
How, and when, did I offend you so much?
My Dear Lord, please explain."

I need not explain anything to you!
How dare you question my plan!
Do you think that you can anticipate me?
I was here before the void began.

You offer me your songs and praises
Wanting mighty miracles in return
Then the rest of the week you deny and shun me
And expect me not to feel spurned.

Where were you when I built Alpha Centauri?
Do you know why my insects have lived so long?

Have you seen the view?
From the sixth moon of the Globus Nebulae?
Or the beings who live in the diamond rocks of Patong?
Do you think what you see is all there is?
Some things are worth more than your praises and songs.

If you truly believed in me
There'd be no hopelessness in your mind
I do know what was and what will be
And I can save the future from behind.
So, go away and weep no more
The future is what I decide it to be
There will be another tomorrow
As long as I decide it will be.

Tell me, sweet lord
Why you turned your back on me?
Tell me, sweet lord
Will it be for eternity?
Tell me, tell me, sweet lord, just
Tell me till I understand
Tell me, sweet lord
Is this part of your master plan?

Tell me, sweet lord
Tell me what I've done wrong
Tell me, tell me, sweet lord
Why redemption is taking so long?
Tell me, tell me, sweet lord, just
Give me a little sign

Tell me, sweet lord
Is this pain something divine?

Tell me, sweet lord
How long this has got to last?
Tell me, sweet lord
How long I have got to fast?
Tell me, tell me, sweet lord, just
Tell me till I understand
Tell me, sweet lord
That it is part of your master plan.

An Awesome Loving God

What is it like to be immortal?
To live for infinity
To see time and space as an irrelevance
Created, just for life to be.

Time and space are like the number eight
Has no beginning or no end
Moves from the very large to the very small
Just as the Lord intends.

The void was created so that the universe could be
In the vast darkness before time appears
When he lived for a trillionth of a second
Or a trillion trillion years.

And he looked at the empty, expanding universe
Whose only purpose was to change
It knew nothing but the darkness of the void
And he decided that things he would rearrange.

And God created light so that the universe could see itself,
Created life to stop it being alone
Created time so that things could evolve and grow
Created love to keep it all in tone.

And the universe evolved and grew
And God knew that it would be good
Out of the deep, deep love, He created man
And made sure, upright, he stood.

Upright we stand, and we have free will
To do what's right or wrong
To blaspheme, cheat, kill or maim
Or praise God in a song.
The God of the Old Testament was a jealous God
Who used His power in a truly impressive way
Who can forget Noah and the Ark?
Most of Earth's life and humanity swept away

Then, out of that deep, deep love, He sent His only son
To wipe away our earthly sins
To allow us to find redemption
To make sure His children win

Out of that deep, deep love
He still leaves us with free will
And He watches while we abuse the power
He watches while we kill each other,
Cheat, maim, enslave, and lie
And, yet, He loves us still.

How great thou art, my loving God
Mine armour and my shield
I come in love to worship you
And to you, I truly yield.

SONGS OF INSIGHT AND WISDOM

I am not pretending to be wise, nor am I suggesting that I have a great insight into anything.

To me, wisdom comes from an in-depth analysis of all the facts about a wide range of ideas over an extended period. Knowledge and insight come through the osmosis process.

I have given some things great thoughts, and through that process, I believe I have gained a view on certain things.

Sometimes there is a disconnect between the absolute certainties of the brain and the innermost uncertainties of the heart.

Sometimes you have to decide whether taking a good look all around is more useful than simply going full speed ahead with those blinkers on.

These poems reflect my certainties—right here, right now.

Futile Objectives

We met in a race
A race of great pace
Frail and fragile was I.
You had your blinkers on
And you could do a ton
And I was just living a lie.

I fell at the first hurdle
You were still going strong at the last
And I never saw what became of you.
With no blinkers on, I could see all around
But you only had one view.

At the end of the race
The race of great pace
I was talking to a friend in the bar.
Halfway through a conversation
Of no particular direction
I asked what became of the star.

The friend said as far as he knew
Your ambition just grew
And the race was just another hurdle to you.

With those blinkers on...
You're still going strong
And you were last heard of ...
In Timbuktu.

Footprints in a Sandstorm

How fragile the links of certainty
How tenuous the connections in time
Humanity ... and all its achievements
Are simply footprints in the sandstorm
Of evolution.

From Creation to Big Bang
When the universes were just ... spaces,
Awaiting the enigmatic, circuitous ...
Time.

That period lasted for either a trillionth of
A trillionth of a second
Or a trillion trillion years
No time, no blackholes...
No past, no present ... no future...

But ... a God.

For 'IT'... was there before time ...
At Creation.
Before ... the spaces created meaning on a page
Before ... silence created meaning in a word

Before ... death created life
Before ... fire created water.

In the beginning, there was the space
And this space evolved ...
Into God.

And God created time ... and humanity ...
And sandstorms
And footprints.

Questions Along A Tortured Path

I wonder where along your tortured path
Did the light from your essence go dim?
Where, oh where, along this journey so short
Did you decide you did not want to swim?

How could it happen, this seamless change?
Was it at the beginning, before your birth?
When you first glimpsed the life ahead,
Looked at the conclusions of your future
And buried your self-worth.

When did you decide you had no value, no visibility, no light?
Who made your recipe for survival so frail?
An emaciating, finite spiral to oblivion
With no senses, no judgement, no notion to review your trail.

What must it be like to be afraid of harmless shadows?
Insecurity, like raw, unhealable, forever painful sores.
Your soul dying, because a stranger did not say hello.
Your heart crying because no one opens the doors.

How do you exist, with an ego so unsure of itself?
How do you take the day, sleep, wake, and brave another?

Continually looking for the eagerly awaited slight
And having perceived it, go any further.

Can we grow from a seed so distorted?
Will we ever turn into a tree, strong and true?
You have to find your own answers and solutions,
In the end, as at the beginning, it is all up to you.

The Results Could Be Tragic

I sat there probing resolutely behind
The elaborate protection of a feather tough mind
What I finally perused made no initial sense
What stared back at me was virginal innocence

I must say, at first, I was genuinely bemused
Then fear hit me at how easily this mind could be used
With a body so strong and a mind so lethargic
In the wrong hands, the results could be tragic

The mind said it didn't really like to think
Because it could never really see the link
Between analysing what the media say
And just trying to survive for another day

So, it goes home, sits down, eat and watch TV
Questions nothing, just believe what it sees
If they say plutonium dust is good for the pup
The next day, it will try to get some from the shop

It says it is disillusioned with the progress of its life
But what can it do when political excess is so rife?
You cannot win, so what's the sense of the fight?
It's best to ignore it; everything will be all right

So, it just goes along, giving up all of its rights
While the power of the state develops a real hard bite
There is no one to question and keep it in control
And the minds are too busy doing as they are told

The mind said it didn't like the independent press
Because to read them it's like an intelligence test
Besides, they never inform it what it has to do
And there is no bingo on page twenty-two

At that point of the probe, it started to sleep
It was only nine-thirty, but the sleep was deep
I came out of that mind. Totally perplexed.
And I am just wondering, what's going to happen next?!

Retrospectively Yours—From 1985

So ... this is 1985
And I am still alive
How many years to go
That, I just don't know,
But ... this is nineteen eighty-five
And ... I am still alive
I've got to thank God for getting me through
To this year that is so new
Only as I look ahead, I really can't see
How ... I am going to get through.

When I was a boy a long time ago
I used to have lots of dreams
Now ... they are still in my head
But they have all failed
And all I have are silent screams.

Back in Hambrooks, when life was so plain
A doctor I wanted to be
I came to England, the land of hope
The land of prosperity.
They put me in a class
The class was last.

But that was no reason to give in
All I had to do was fight, and I would get through
Cos I am a fish, and I can swim.

The reality hit me in 65
Twenty years ago, tonight
When I realised that dream was gone,
And if I wanted to survive, I had to swim.
So, I took some time, joined the Navy
I went and saw the world
Went here, there and everywhere and met all kinds of girls.
At a point in that time, in the South China Sea
A serious thought came to me
It said what will you be doing in seventy-five?
And that far ahead, I couldn't see
So, I said fine, let's get out of here
Self-discipline ... that's what I have got
Cannot hang about, must get out
A sailor, I am not.
So, like a lot of my friends, who happened to be black
We all got disillusioned and left
Came out the Navy, lost in this world
The nation's uncaring attitude left us bereft.

So, I went on a course
And I always came first
And I really thought I was the best
Joined the big company in seventy-two
My friend ... all the skies were blue
Twelve years have gone
Promotion I've had one

And in my mind, I feel I am the best
Best at whatever I do
They all say that's true
But in reality, I am just one of the rest.

The dreams I had ... well, they have not disappeared
They just have not appeared
And I am left in this limbo
Not knowing which way to go
Or ... even if I want to go.
I cannot see the road ahead
I cannot see the way through
I don't even know if I can make it
Ambition or not that's true.

Ambitious am I, millionaire I wanted to be,
By the time I was forty-three
I am thirty-six now, holy cow,
Forty-three is no longer an eternity.
In seven years, I have to do
What I have not done in thirty-two
And I don't know if I can do it anymore
Or what's in store.

Well, it is nineteen eighty-five
And I am still alive
I have got strength, and I've got my wits
I am going to take up the pieces and twist them around
And turn the pieces into bits.

SONGS OF LOVE
AND LONGING

This collection is about love.

The joy of love, the pain of love, the humour of love, the insecurity of love. The longing that comes from waiting for the conditions to appear that make you sure you're doing the right thing.

Love shows itself at moments when you least expect it. When you are thinking of something else. It creeps up on you sometimes and makes you realise that something in your life is different and will never be the same again.

The love of family is reflected in this collection, and sibling love is one of the great emotional drivers in life.

There is a longing for certainty to appear, for the emotions to settle, for indecision to go to bed and stay there.

Love is sometimes painful and can sometimes make you run away and never fall for it again.

And yet, we hunger for it always.

This collection pays homage to the idea of love and its consequences.

One Shot At Redemption

My lady went and left me
Left me for another plan
What was hard for me to understand
She didn't leave me for another man

And when I asked the reason
The tears just filled her eyes
She said although I loved and needed you
You couldn't give me paradise

She said
I get one shot at redemption
And I can't afford to lose
I get one shot at redemption
And I had to choose
She said
I get one shot at redemption
And for us, it is bad news
I get one shot at redemption
No more pain and blues

After three years of courtship
Four years of wedded bliss

This was unexpected
Her love I was going to miss

I said
What about the future?
And all those long-term schemes
What about the children?
Who filled up all our dreams

She said
I get one shot at redemption
And I can't afford to lose
I get one shot at redemption
And I had to choose
I get one shot at redemption
And for us, it is bad news
I get one shot at redemption
No more pain and blues

She went off to start her new life
And I stayed home to think
When it got near to breaking point
I had one or two to drink

After the divorce I got smart
And started to take stock
Just when I started to enjoy myself
She wanted to come back

I said
I get one shot at redemption

And I can't afford to lose
I get one shot at redemption
And I had to choose
I get one shot at redemption
And for us, it is bad news
I get one shot at redemption
No more pain and blues.

Lady Prime

I met her in her summer years
Her beauty transcended all time
She was wide-eyed in her innocence
Gently simmering in her prime

Her youthful zest ... and joy of life
Eroded all my cynical years
The sweetness of her inner self
Filled my eyes with tears

She is always there for me
Only whispers when I expected a scream
Seemed to need me just as she met me
My cup overfloweth ... is it a dream?

Stay by my side ... Lady Prime
Don't wander too far from my view
There are many things I like in this universe
But I really ... truly ... do love you.

Focus

Ah...you could have said...
You were getting wed
And telling me goodbye.
There could have been a hint...
That the love had a tint
And there were no more tears left to cry.

Was it a game...?
Or was I insane?
Believing...I was sharing your dream.
You could still have been queen...
I wouldn't have created a scene
For I love you too much, it would seem.

There are moments in time...
When without reason or rhyme
You're the total focus of my mind.
I seem to close my eyes...
Only to realise
That...invisibly...
Mentally...
Achingly...
You've been standing there...
All the time.

It Really Would Be Nice

I know it's hard...but...

It really would be nice
If you just went with the flow
To let your insecurities, go to sleep
As not all problems will cause you woe

It really would be nice
To take life as it comes
To see yourself as part of the jigsaw
Created by Mother Nature's womb
It really would be nice

It really would be nice
If life was just a slow ... slow dream
Which went exactly as you planned
Or you could get off in midstream

It really would be nice
If your lover's realities were tailor-made
If our problems came in micro size
And their solutions macro grade

It really would be nice
If you trusted my words a little more
And not take my absence
As something else to store

It really will be nice
When you accept all that I have to be
The totality of my life so far
Shapes and makes my reality

If I told you that I loved you,
Would you ask me why?
If I told you because I needed you
Would you still ask me why?
If I said because you were my missing side
Would you say, don't lie?
If I said I tell the truth
Would it make you cry?

Cry into the midnight cup
Sweet bird full of youth
Come ... wrap yourself in merriment
Come ... wrap yourself in joy
Go...tell the sweet tomorrow
That love is here at last

Come and fill my senses
With potions rich and pure
But...when you walk beside me
Then you must be sure

Why does she hesitate?
What thoughts run through the petrified forest?
What force holds her...in its vicelike grip?
Afraid to move forward...afraid to look back.
Why does she wait?
Like a phoenix awaiting new birth

If only she could come...a little closer
Then I'd be able to touch...hold...
And finally, bring her to the safety of my love.
But standing there...
On the precipice called indecision
I cannot save her
Without killing myself.

Memories Of Childhood

I have so many memories of my childhood,
Each one so vivid and clear.
They are like giant, but silent mahoe trees
Dominating the landscapes of my dreams.
Seeing all, and yet so large
They are almost invisible.

The recollections are almost Omni-prescient
Using prophetic words just like a mantic
Referring me back to a distant past
And showing me a far-off future
All at the same time.

And each night I travel back to the forest,
With bamboo leaves on the ground
Cushioning my fall, as the branch
I was hoping to clasp on the way down
Escapes my grasp yet again.
I fall into the eiderdown of the bamboo leaves
And I am safe once more.

In the noon of the day
We go scrumping for mangoes

On the farms, hanging off the sides
Of the Blue Mountain.
Unafraid in our arrogance,
We think no harm can come of us.

The farmer sees us coming yet again,
The fifth time for the week.
He sharpens his machete across the stone
And looks at us in glee.

"Come," he says with his eyes
"I dare you to come," he stares
Hands akimbo, cutlass blade ready to strike
He hopes our arrogance will cease.

I am sitting at the top of the tree.
And I gauge how far it is to the ground.
I am calculating how many branches I will need to swing on
To avoid his slashing blade.
He spies me in the tree,
He thinks he knows the only thing I can do.
He moves over to where he imagines I will land,
And I busily recalculate.

We stay motionless for an eternity.
Both waiting for the moment to strike.
Me, the nearest branch of the tree
And him, wherever his machete lands.

My young brother and my cousin shouts and run past him,
And his blade swings in their direction.

I know he is now distracted,
And I make my first move to land.
I swing to one branch going East, and he follows.
I catch another bough going West, and he is lost
My last branch still goes West, and he is defeated.
I land, roll forward and run in one all-encompassing move.

The four of us just kept running
Until Church Hill came into view
By now the poor farmer had given up the chase
Paused under a Star Apple tree and smiled
Caught the cool breeze as it bounced off the mountain
Job done for another day.

And these memories keep coming back to me
Reminding me of who I am
I smile as I remember My Jamaica
And like the giant Iroko of my African Ancestors
The Mahoe tree smiles back at me.

SONGS FOR THE SILVER YEARS

I am getting old. No doubt about it.

I look in the mirror, and I look OK, not as young as I remember, but passable. My body is changing. Daily, monthly, yearly it seems to move to another place, and sometimes I cannot even remember where I have been.

With all the tablets I now take to keep alive, my body looks out of place in my head. I always see myself with a body that is moving. The way to stay alive is to keep moving. Once you stop, it seems all the past mistakes catch up with you and bury you.

There was a time when I was proud of my physical self. It had dexterity; it had mobility, and it had a physical presence, which kept me safe. My physicality was unchallengeable and powerful.

Now, all I have when I look are outlines that show what and where I once was. The contours are now flabby, and there is only enough power to help me survive, as opposed to letting me live.

And as I come to terms with the new me, I find the journey from one state to the next challenging.

These two songs reflect the journey.

Managing the Incline

I am fifty-six years of age old man
And my mind is not at ease
The messengers are coming in thick and fast
And my destiny cannot be appeased

We are all born with a billion breaths
And my heart has been beating too fast
And as you know, I have not been sitting there counting
So I have no idea how long it is all going to last

They say it is not the breaths you have
But what you achieve in between
Only sometimes like footprints in a sandstorm
The results can never be seen

The incline is getting steeper
The blood flows ever so freely now
As I sit here reminiscing
There is something I will avow

I will not sit there in a wheelchair
Looking out of my window into a brook
Living my days behind the net curtains
Like some seedy little crook

I will not be sitting in some wheelchair
Waiting for my next oxygen fix
Blood too tired to move anything
Swallowing my chemical mix

I cannot sit there in the wheelchair
Waiting for the next cough to slay
All my dreams of a better tomorrow
By stealing my next breath away

The infections are now on a rota
Ear first and then the chest
Itchy skin, headaches, and blood-filled phlegm
To keep me at my best

It is the little things
Like running upstairs to the loo,
It's not major; it's not significant
I mean, it's not like walking to Timbuktu

Is it all part of an incline?
In man's journey from and back to the void
Should I be a little more philosophic?
Instead of so blindingly annoyed.

There Is No Pain

There is no pain, there is no pain
But the red river flows deeply outside my veins
The crustaceous pulmonary fibroids open to create a pathway
The chemical dam weakens and gives up in vain
But there is no pain, there is no pain.

There is no pain, there is no pain
Not intense pain
Not the pain from an ablated heart
That leaves you just wanting to die
The stomach cramp holds you in its grip
The fingers refuse to bend and stay stiffened like I have no joints
But there is no pain, there is no pain.

And in the far distance the sound of winter,
Like a remorseless express train,
Whistles its intention to end the summer reign
And it tells you it is on its way
The coughs are surlier now, not so easy to fob off
They stick to the inner membranes
And need more muscular energy to bring them up

The breath runs out of vigour and refuses to return

It just hangs there, like an unfinished question
And in the ensuing battle, between my lungs and my heart,
The red river flows deeply outside my veins
And my body, accustomed to the sounds and what they bring,
Becomes anxious in the impending anticipation of doom
But there is no pain, there is no pain.

SONGS OF
REFLECTION

The road to wisdom is a long and tortuous one. I think that a man who seeks wisdom for his own requirements will not get it. Knowledge is attained for passing on ideas to the next generation. Keeping it to yourself is contra indicative of sense.

These songs are about journeys. My reflections imagine how things were, are, and could be.

The Traveller

She was travelling through the forbidden land,
Too confused to think.
There were no clues for her to understand,
That there was no missing link.

There were dried minds splattered on the ground,
And lifeless thoughts untold.
She wondered as she looked around,
How the story would unfold.

How happy was that Sunday morn?
As she laid in that bed.
Waiting for her child to be born,
Nine months after she was wed.

The TV kept warning of some modern danger,
That nobody understood,
It kept saying to watch that stranger,
Who everyone misunderstood.

The warning went out all the time,
Till it lost its point.
No one would believe that such a crime,
Could this world, disjoint.

There was a flash, a bang, and then a light,
And then all hell broke loose.
The world stood still and gasped at the sight,
And then quickly tightened the noose.

How she escaped, she would never ever know,
But escape she did.
The baby she had would never ever grow,
That thought she always hid.

London was a mass of forbidden pain,
Nine million people died.
Birds and planes came down like rain,
And even rivers dried.

The city's buildings were empty shells,
Like skeletons, they stood.
The opera died at Saddler's Wells,
Just as it was getting good.

There was no more football at Hackney Marsh,
Just a load of dust.
The remains of humans, like some unused starch,
Was blown away by a gust.

Westminster, that great seat of power,
Disintegrated in a flash.
The rest of London went in that hour,
Like a window without a sash.

The thing that really grasped her mind,

Was that she was all alone.
No bus, no car, no movement she could find,
She was on her own.

The frustration of the inability to find,
How and why it all began.
Played havoc on her inner mind,
Was it all because of man?

No More Tears from Baghdad

The little boy sat there without a soul
His eyes saw nothing but pain
His ears heard every gunshot
Again and again and again.

He saw his father taken away
He watched his mother die
He stared as the last breath escaped her lips
And all he could say was, "Why?"

He kept remembering his first day at the orphanage
He just kept looking for his mum and dad
In the halls, the kitchen, the bedrooms
Their absence almost drove him mad.

It was in his eighth year, the madness came
When all hope had left him alone
Finally, finally, he had to admit
That he was on his own.

He said he blamed the Americans
And I can't say I blame him at all
It is so sad to see so little forgiveness
In the eyes of one so small.

And I looked again in his eyes
And the pupils no longer shine
The absence of hope has deadened the gaze
I am so glad he is not an enemy of mine.

Communication

Sometimes I wish we were dumb,
And we didn't have to talk.
Then nothing would be misconstrued,
And our meanings would be stark.

I mean, take this situation,
I say to you, "Hello."
You twist it in your 'educated' mind,
And come up with, "Hell, no."

Now that wasn't what I said,
Or even meant to say.
But that's communication,
In this world today.

People running blind,
Self-doubt racking their brain.
Afraid if they listen too closely,
Their (outdated) beliefs might wane.

Individuals have no thought,
They keep on reading 'The Sun'.
Which 'Mirrors' their empty minds,
And keeps them on the run.

Oh, if only we would listen,
And understand every word.
East and West might stop their war,
Nah, that is too absurd!

My Words, My Lines

I am trying to be a poet
I am trying to write what I think
I want my lines to have meaning
To put a little smile in your mind
To make you say, "Well, I didn't see that coming,"
Not all the time, but just now and then.

I don't want my lines to be transparent
I am not writing a weather report
I am not thinking of a formal document
I want some of my lines to be devious and mischievous
Taking you on a journey you've never been on before
I want you to wake up in the middle of the night saying…
"I get it, I get it… That's what he meant."

I do not want to spend all my time
Writing fluffy, fluffy rhymes
And all that's left is the rhyme and no other sense of purpose.
Now and again, God knows, I need a little prose
To let the words dance and sing in universal harmony
To hear the cadence ring out as one word
Interact with the next and as if by magic
Synergy manifesting and magnifying itself.

I do not always want to write complex quatrains
Where words can mean everything and nothing
Where history can be rewritten again and again
And the writer can never be wrong.

I want my words to take you on a journey
I want them to meander about a bit; take you here, take you there
And when you think that's it
You suddenly find that the lines are taking you
Backwards and forward at the same time
Up and down, left and right, creating paintings in your mind.
You see my words create the vehicle
That drives you ever so slowly to my heart
And finally, my soul.

If Tomorrow Comes

If Tomorrow Comes
And finds me in its path
I pray it meets me satiated
And not still full of wrath
I hope I will not be unsatisfied
Displeased with what I have done
With all the time I was given
To move the battle on.

If Tomorrow Comes
And we are still learning forgiveness and peace
Whilst some people's abandoned humanity
Keeps the world ill at ease
I hope I will not be unsatisfied
Displeased with what I have done
With all the time I was given
To move the battle on.

If Tomorrow Comes
And Gaia is still shedding her tears
For the landscape that is dying from greed
Whilst the Oligarchs laugh at her fears
I hope I will not be unsatisfied

Displeased with what I have done
With all the time I was given
To move the battle on.

And when tomorrow comes
And the imagined realities fall from our eyes
And we see just what we have done
It will be a positive surprise.
I hope I will not be unsatisfied
Displeased with what I have done
With all the time I was given
To move the battle on.

I Had These Thoughts Sometimes

I had these thoughts sometimes before,
On random days and random ways
They seemed to capture and enrapture me
Making me forever seeking more.

I had these feelings sometimes in the past
On perchance weeks and perchance aspects
They hold me in their vice-like and ice-like grip
But I know they cannot last.

I have these visions of a future time
On happenstance years filled with happenstance tears
I am filled with prophecy, things that I foresee
But none of them is worth a dime.

I am in the now, the only real moment of veracity
On a second of time, where all is sublime
I am pacing the act. I am chasing the fact.
To laugh at and ridicule opacity.

COVID So Vivid

I am sitting here thinking of COVID
And I am trying to be kind
Watching peace in its dream-like state
Trying to find its mind

I am trying to be positive
Trying to give nature the benefit of doubt
And as the death rate gets higher and so much higher
I'm wondering what it is all about.

Is nature trying to tell us something?
Trying to give us a clue
Finally, running out of patience
And will now do what it has to do

I have heard that humanity will never change
Until it is right upon the edge
It will still be overconfident
Until it is on the ledge

I am filled with gratitude
That the horsemen have not yet called
That the vaccines may arrive just in time
Before COVID takes us all

I am trying to maintain my humour
Using sarcasm and irony to cover the sighs
Laughing until my belly hurts.
And wiping the tears from my eyes

Like I say;
I am still sitting here thinking of COVID
And I am trying to be kind
Watching peace in its dream-like state
Trying to find its mind.

Sheep Attacking Wolves

He stood there shouting in his quiet way,
Trying to get safely through another day,
Aggressively failing to see the power gulf,
It was like watching a sheep attacking a rabid wolf.

He was trying to show that he knew his job,
But all he was showing me was the size of his gob.
Everyone listened as he tried to explain,
It was then I decided to step into the terrain.

I said to him; I felt he was attacking me,
And failing to explain himself, miserably.
If he had checked his notes, he would have seen his mistake,
Come back to me when you know the answer, for heaven's sake.

His courage buckled he went into a shell.
His face crumpled as the wolf pinpointed the smell.
He started to blabber, but I, the wolf, broke the spell,
Grabbed hold of his bullshit and dragged him to hell.

PART TWO

The Long Songs

Content

The Long Songs

These songs could not be contained in twenty-five lines. There were so many things to say in them. They are the culmination of long thoughts and reflections, sometimes over years. They cover journeys of centuries or deep, deep journeys of acceptance. I call them my 'Journey Songs'.

Sharm El Sheik was started in Egypt in 2010 and finally finished in 2015. This poem is about acceptance and the battle between hope and hopelessness.

The Lamentations of the Chauffeur, the Taxi Driver and the Submariner is about ill health and walking alongside death and seeing it right up close in others and yourself, and still maintaining some kind of dignity.

Life is about the journey from the cradle to the grave and finding who you are.

The Black Man's Song is a poetic and epic odyssey into the African diaspora from 1450 to 2016.

Stay Focused ends the journey with my version of *Desiderata*.

And it is still a beautiful world.

The Ascension of Hopelessness

The town centre is desolate, dismal, dying from decline
Paddy Power and the rest of the gang are in charge
On every corner, on every bend,
Their welcoming lights flashing,
They fight the pound shops for supremacy.
The beggar goes from one to another
Earnestly begging a quid for a meal
The gambler fights him for the pound
To feed his pointless greed

The migrant wonders why he travelled so far
To taste this barren fruit
He has spent all his money to get here
From a land where the sun always shone
And the heat was something to shun
Now he has no money to go home
And begs forgiveness for getting it wrong.

He would gladly face death in his homeland
To pick a free mango once more
He has imprisoned himself in this, the free land
And has nowhere else to turn.

The High Road looks worn out and threadbare
Even the lights have seen better days
The once shiny bronze of the lampstands
Have succumbed to the oxidised green of neglect

And the powerless still needs something to hold on to
Still thinks the super-rich is perturbed
Still thinks he is part of a caring society
That cares whether he lives or die.

The super-rich gangs with their ancestral homes
Scoop up the money from the poor
They ensure that nothing is left for anyone else
After all, they, the privileged might just need it one day.

And the middle still think they can reach the top
Because once in a while one of them does.
Everyone thinks it will be them
But only once in a while, someone does.

Meanwhile, on the outskirts of Elysium
A drug mule stabs her rival for turf
No role model has ever come to show her the way
And she has given up hoping for a better day
In the highest spires of that extraordinary place
A privileged wealthy junkie impatiently sits
He keeps going to the gold-framed window
To see if the mule has delivered his fix.

He wonders where the mule has gone
How dare her wastes his precious time

He makes a phone call to his uptown dealer
And another mule gets on his bike.
The junkie will never get stabbed
The dealer will never even get recognised
The mule will last about five years
And another mother will wipe her tears.

And Capitalism wakes and lazily scan his domain
Smiles as he gets dressed for the day
Looks at the upper floors of skyscrapers
Filled with his unsuspecting slaves
But looks no further down.

Anansi Nuh Come Yah Fe Ramp

Dem drag me people across the Sea
Frighten Dem into forgetting me
My heart cried when I glimpsed their pain
An I swear it nah goh happen again
Cause Anansi nuh come ova yah fe ramp.

I am a God,
A laughing, joking, peaceful God
The God of lyrics, the God of Rhymes
The God who was being worshipped
From way back in ancient times

I got too comfortable,
being worshipped for the stories I had to tell
I forgot this was a world of struggle
A world of greed
Whilst some of my people were being dragged to hell

You know what it is like
In the middle of the tale
You are so wrapped up in the twist and turn
That when you catch yourself
Half of your audience has disappeared.

You look and thrash around blindly

Almost as if you are a pea in a tiny pod
Mi seh, Me should have seen it coming
For I am Anansi, the story God.

Where was I in 1441
When the Portuguese came to Cabo Branco
Kidnapped 20 from my audience
Took them to Portugal as slaves
And I was too busy to feel the loss.

I did not see it coming
Portugal was just
A small place trying to look big.
Should have peered into the future
To see how big, it would become

Eighth of August 1444 was a bad day
235 stolen by the Portuguese De Freitas
And still, I took no notice
Did not even hear the screams
Too busy enthralling my audience
With stories of unachievable dreams

I first became aware in 1485
When news came in from Elmina
That Diogo da Azambuja was building a castle
A slave trading fort in the heart of my land.
I just did not know what was to come.
I am ashamed
I am a God, a Deity, Powerful,
Capable of all that is necessary

To make what I want, real
I just did not believe what was to come.

For 10,000 years I was the master
Using stories to maintain my will
Enemies had given up trying to destroy me
And I had grown unfit and blind
In the absence of any foe.

My people were safe
They roamed the land in peace
Gathering in the market squares, the valleys
The riverbanks and forests
To hear the next instalment of my tales.

I vow, I have no more stories to tell
No more tales to while away the day
I swear that I will tell no more parables
No anecdotes will pass from my lips
Until my people are free.

So now I am garnering my raiment of war
My brother and sister gods are gathering too
And we will meet in the halls of Osiris
To do what we know, we must do.

I call on Olorun, Amma, Nyame and Leza
To take care of all that we do
I call on Horus, Kibuka and Ogun
To take charge of our battle cry
Eshu and I will weave the tales

Design cunning strategies to guarantee the win
Osiris will be there to ensure
That the underworld doesn't get filled.

Now, at long last, we are coming across the Atlantic
Into Europe and the Americas, we will land
Coming to rescue our people
From someone else's plan

There is no smile upon my lips
A kind of coldness I store in my heart
We were sent here to learn peace and forgiveness
But the price is too hard to pay
We would have to sacrifice ourselves
To adhere to someone else's
Morality play

A time now fe change, to bring back order
Because the days of peace and forgiveness dem gahn
An if a war dem want, den a so it af fe goh.
Cause Anansi no come yah fe ramp

The Spark (and Its Afterthoughts)

Where did you go, where have you been?
You seem to be lost in the miasma of my uncertainties
If my sudden and untimely death frightened you away
Then please note that I am alive again, so please call
I need you.

Without you, I am just a list of endless possibilities
An obscured pool of things that could be, but won't be,
Things that should be, but can't be
Without you, I am a lifeless cloud of incertitude
An intangible, clarity-free, soulless edifice incapable of actions
Good or bad
I need you.

And, ah, I remember you so well.
I recall your drive, your ideas and your get-up-and-go.
You were the tiny grain of energy that ignited my fire
That converted my listlessness into myopic paths of desire
I need you.

So many things left me that night, never to return it seems.
Sometimes I cannot recall how spiritual I was before the journey
I was alive; I woke up alive again, and the middle is gone,
Never to return.
What route did I take? I do not know.

Did I stop for a cup of tea? I do not know.
I awoke from death, with half of my spirit missing.

Spark, you were just another one of my weapons
That deserted me when the horsemen came calling
Like strength, energy, focus and never say die
You were not there when I woke up.
It seems that you were all too afraid to stay true and loyal.

Or were you all the sacrifice I had to make?
The trade-off made to ensure the certainty of the next breath
The Dane-geld paid to be left alone
If so, then you really ought to have asked me
If the next breath was worth such pain, such uncertainty,
Such intense disillusionment at the mediocrity of what remains.

Afterthoughts

My soul says to me sometimes that I am a spirit having a human experience and that I should not worry, as I will leave all this behind when I return to my spiritual plane. However, I wonder sometimes whether we are bound to go on and on through these experiences until we find the right solution to the paradoxes they create.

For instance, if my soul is here to learn how to manage jealousy, then it may go through several divorces and difficult relationships before it finally conceives how to share non-judgemental, honest and pure love based on trust. The pain of those human physical experiences may be such that they create negative spin-offs, which take millennia for my soul to put back into balance.

Oh spark, I miss you.

Maybe you have been carrying me
When I had no other means of support.
Maybe you are the inspiration behind my every waking hour.
Maybe you are there waiting for me to finally realise that you cannot help me until I choose to help myself. Just patiently standing there in the shade, waiting for me to realise that I have been given a new road to travel and that the map has been in my pocket all the time and all I had to do was look for it, and it would appear,

Along with strength, energy, focus and never say die.

Sharm El Sheik

An old acquaintance of mine came to visit me in Sharm El Sheik
We stopped and exchanged thoughts for a while
I cannot say I was pleased to see him
As he always leaves me with a frenetic smile.

I said I was surprised to see him so far from home
In such a beautiful place
A haven where the sea meets the sky
And blue is the colour of gentle solace.

I normally expect to see him
In a palace of frozen doubts
Or a cauldron of painful memories
Laced with screams and shouts.

I asked if he had travelled so far
Just to idle away some time with me
I explained that I wasn't all that glad to see him
Because of our painful history.

I asked him where his brothers were
As they always seemed to travel in fours
He said they were down the road in Palestine
On another of their unending Middle East tours.

Finally, I said why are you here?
You have brought me nothing but pain
All your stories, myths, half-truths and lies
I just could not listen to them again.

He said sit down and rest your feet
Try and see if you can calm down
I have brought you here to Sharm El Sheik
To replace that age-old frown.

We brothers came to see you ten years ago
And we responded to the prayers to save your life
Finally, I persuaded them to leave you alone
And take that old man and his lonely wife.

I have returned to visit you
To see what you have done with the respite
But all I see is sadness and fear
And a heart that's full of spite.

I see a man so full of pride
A heart becoming stone
Your head was meant to see the stars
But suspicion is all you've grown.

Have you seen the sunset in Sharm El Sheik?
The way the yellow dies and orange calls
The way the orange sacrifices itself so that brown can live
And then darkness descends on it all.

That is the journey of all that lives

From the beginning to the end of time
And like the sun, my ageing son,
You will be taken at your prime.

But...not yet the brothers have told you
Not yet is the plan for you
Just look around and observe the land
And get to know what you can do.

It is ten years since any rain
Has fallen on this barren land
Yet the green shoots of life are everywhere
Like a part of some master plan.

The hot breeze rustles across your skin
And soothes it like a gentle cream
The big red sea, so warm and blue
Just like a little stream.

The sand is in the foreground
It is here, there and everywhere
It defines all that you can do
From here to Timbuktu.

Despite all its adversity
Sharm El Sheik still wears a smile
No one would ever know it's in pain
Because it carries it all with style.

You do not carry your pain with style
You carry it on your chin

You carry it in your deadened eyes
And in your down-turned grin.

You carry it in your hopeless stare
And in your withered gait
I am beginning to see an absence of hope
And I pray I am not too late.

Take a look at your wife snorkelling like an innocent child
Seeing, tasting, touching, feeling everything
Almost as if she thinks it's her last day on this planet
And she has to gulp it all in at once.

You were her inspiration
In her dark days, she got reassurance from your smile
She sought solace in your quiet, calm ways
And she has not seen them for a while.

All she gets is your angry stare
And your whining disgruntlement
Constantly,
I mean constantly moaning about everything
And picking those arguments.

She sees things in an uncomplicated way
Life is just to enjoy
Keep it all simple, keep it true
Like a little child with their toy.
But you want to make it all serious
Everything just has to be dark
It must be paranoid and mysterious
Instead of just having a lark.

And in her darkest time of doubt
When she views the road ahead
She wonders if it's worth the ride
With you by her side
Or maybe someone else instead.

Sometimes I glimpse your oldest child
Still searching for his stolen childhood
Still bearing the scars from the pain, you gave him
And yet still seeing in you nothing but good.

He is just beginning to turn things around
I can still see the anger in his eyes
When he remembers how you left him on his own
When he was not yet fully formed.

You were all he had that could
Have helped him shape his world
Yet you abandoned him half-grown.

Your youngest son looks into your eyes
He knows what he is seeking from you
Yet the reassurance he needs, you do not give
Because you are feeling blue.

He wants you to be so proud of him
He has achieved it all to make you proud
Now he is getting disenchanted
Getting fed up with your angry stares

And may
One day

Just walk away
Because he no longer cares.
Your daughter has suffered the worst
She has seldom seen the best of you
She can hardly remember
The laughs, the smiles, the silly jokes
And the loving things that fathers do.

All she sees is moody Dad
Who never seems to smile
Who constantly points out what she does wrong
But seldom what she does in style.

These are not the reasons we saved your life
Not why you are still here
Show us it was worth our while
To keep you living, back there.

You saved my life back there, you sure did
Now I am kept living in a gilded cage
You fill me with steroids and all the other chemical brew
And you still wonder why I am filled with rage.

I was just a simple man
Following a simple plan
Eat to live, not live to eat
Was something simple even I could understand.

Now you leave me with a body that doesn't quite work
A heart too fat to heave
A lung that cannot generate enough air
For me to bob and weave.

I was born a warrior
Born to act
Not used to living in a frozen chair
Not used to being locked in a panic-looking haze
Because my body cannot generate air.

It's been ten years since you abandoned me here
And each day, I am slowly, unerringly, systematically getting worse
You have taken all my positive surge
And obliterated it with reality's curse.

You expect me to be grateful
I am not quite sure what for
You want my thanks and praises
For an engine that doesn't purr.

They say it's seven years of famine for seven years of plenty
And my famine years now add up to ten
And I wake up happy, expecting to see plenty,
But all I get is famine again.

You expect me to be positive
But you have left me armourless in this fight
Meanwhile, the chemical warriors attack me
Leaving me afraid to face another night.

I have sacrificed all my courage
The Dane-geld I paid just to stay alive
It was nine times the ICD shocked my heart
Nine times death called, and I refused to open the door

Nine times the shock lifted me off the bed
Until I couldn't take any more.

My neighbour sat there, staring in a trance
Scratching his head to keep out the thoughts
Waiting for the ambulance to rescue him
From me and my overwhelming pain.

Your steroids leave me with an ungainly size
Which complicates my gait
The chemo tablets and the other sixteen pills
Make death something I contemplate
The constant flu, the constant colds
From one week to the next
The lack of air
The apoplectic stare
As I fight to suck in my next breath.

And in the stillness of the early morn
When the only voice I hear is the one in my head
When all of my organs are in perfect unison,
My rhythms and breaths playing music to my heart
My pacemaker feels like it has also gone to sleep
Leaving my body to play its original part.

I hear a moan of dissatisfaction
Slip-sliding its way into my conscious self
I wonder if I am part of the obvious dream
Coming from the other side of the bed
I wonder what she really thinks
Behind that fulsome smile
How long can she be patient? How long can she be true?
When all she gets is my sullen gloom
And words that are often vile.

And each year I see the small changes
That move things on from the last
Each year I see the colder eyes
That was not there in the past
And I watch in total helplessness
As the cold moves from the eyes down to the mouth
And now those once incessant lips
Just seem to be always closed
The jaws seem to be clenching her teeth
Which widens the flare in her nose.

And early in the morning,
Two strangers lie awake in the bed
Wondering what will become of them
In the coming years ahead.
Will she be a very young, but free widow?
Or a bitter but loyal wife?
Will he find his own salvation? Will he come to terms?
Or just fade away to oblivion and give his wife a life?

And then I wake and watch helplessly as my family grow
Too tired to play my part
The inability to partake or even share
Just leaves me with a broken heart.

And as I look at Sharm El Sheik
It looks back at me with saddened eyes
It shakes its head in disappointment
When it looks at my demise.

Don't patronise me, Sharm El Sheik,
Sitting there in your monotone brown

While foreigners trample all over you
Because you have forgotten how to even frown.

Your beautiful body is trampled on
By tourists who really don't care

Whether Sharm El Sheik still exists
In another twenty years.

And still, you smile your powerless smile
Dreaming of bygone days
When you were the master of the universe
And had skills that still amaze.

The brazen sun rises early in the morning
It leaves no shade in its path
It moves remorselessly across the land
Like a god that's full of wrath.

By midday in the summer months
The sun is a raging cauldron of heat
Even the flies, the roaches and the ants
Have decided to do a full retreat.

And as you gingerly enter the noonday sun
You feel like a traveller in a barren land
The unearthly beat, the unending heat
As you tiptoe into the water from the sand.

And my acquaintance looked puzzlingly at me
As I gazed trance-like at Sharm El Sheik
He started to reminisce about bygone days

And long-gone ways
And some old story about a lake.
I said listen to me, you impatient old man,
I still have part of my story to tell
Let me explain what fills me with pain
And when I am finished,
You can drag me down to hell.

Some people live on a positive plane
Leaving others to take the negative strain.
They avoid all issues that may cause them grief
While others have to bear them, again and again.

They never see problems, so there is no pain
Life is just like drifting down an easy stream
Flipping from one pleasantry to the next
Eating sweet marshmallows and fondant cream.

In the meantime, others are opening the doors
Clearing up the mess left behind by the fondant cream
Fixing the house, making sure the rent gets paid
And making the raft to navigate that stream.

There is very little point explaining how anything works
As nothing can be understood by them, except your visible futility,
And yet they do not do it intentionally
Their ignorance of how the universe works are to blame
They see simplicity and complexity
As one thing and the same.

Lifelines have never dared to approach their countenance
The face is as carefree as virgin snow

Meanwhile, all around them, the supporters are dying
From the strain of producing the daily show.

There is no point seeking reassurance from the void
As it simply cannot understand anyone else's pain
So, you just internalise your thoughts
And let the loneliness and solitude remain.

The horseman looked at me with those saddened eyes
That have seen death and rebirth over and over again
He said nothing for a long time
Whilst I managed my wearisome pain
Finally, when he saw that I was at ease,
He continued with his refrain.

Only this time, as I gazed into his wizened eyes
I felt compassion for the very first time.

He took my hand, and he rubbed the back
As if he was trying to keep me from harm
Only his action in the noonday heat
Made my body feel warm.

Then he said:
"You've got to find yourself another voice
With more hope than the one you use
You've got to find another voice
Here are some options from which you can choose
Even in death, there is hope
But your voice will not be heard
If in the heat of the battle for survival

You show that you cannot cope.
Be strong, my young survivor,
Show no fear in your heart
Find yourself another voice

And let it play its part."

Let the voice be strong as the rocks on the edge of the shore
Let the voice be as powerful as the wind that blows and blows
Let it be as long-lasting as the sand beneath your feet
Let it be as loving as the first suck on your mother's teat
Let it resound, like water from a mighty stream
Let it be as fearless as the warriors in your dreams.
Let it be as loving as the tears that flow from your eyes
Let it be as gentle as slowly escaping sighs
And when you die, the world will know you lived
Because your resonance will still be loud
It will echo all across Sharm El Sheik
It will boom around London town
The gatherings will be enormous
To remember your great deeds
All will have sad, sad eyes,
Reminisce on bygone days
On all that was achieved,
On your life,
Legacy
Demise.

The Lamentations of the Chauffeur, the Taxi Driver and the Submariner

We sat in the A&E reminiscing about bygone days
On events from our collective past
On things and times that we all shared
But remember from a different point of view.

We talked about the Beatles and the Rolling Stones
Fleetwood Mac and Alan Price, Eric Burdon
The Animals and Georgie Fame
Of the Marquee, Ronnie Scott's and Cue
The Rainbow and Whisky A Go-Go
That's WAGS to me and you.

The Stones concert in Hyde Park in sixty-nine
The Beatles in the Albert Hall
How music is so vital to the young
And reclines as reality starts making the call.

The Chauffeur laughed as he remembered his joyful life
From Bethnal Green to Tenerife
And back to Chigwell
Now he lives quietly in his near resting place
His kids have all done well
He now pays the piper the full fee
For all the scams he's pulled

For all the ruthless misguided decisions he has made
To get himself out of hell.

He lives there in his bloated form
Excesses seeping out of his greasy pores
Heart failure stops him getting fit
And apnea ensures he snores
And yet he laughs in the twilight
As the sun gives up its day
And the moon takes over running things.
He calls himself the 'Fatman.'
Yet there is no irony left in his heart
In his eyes, there is the resentment
Of life's broken promises about immortality
He thought he would be twenty-five forever
That he would live a thousand years and
Die, still looking and feeling twenty-five.

Now he realises that the parts
Can only regenerate seventy times or so, and
Then forever they are gone.
That there is no point living to one hundred and fifty
If your skin has turned to stone
Or worse, simply no longer there.
So, we remembered the great days of the sixties
And prepare for the road ahead.

The Taxi Driver laid there in his hospital crib
So small, you thought he was wearing a bib
Lights flashing, sounds alarming
Telling him constantly that he is ill.

He smiles the smile of the fearful one
He puts on his brave face again
And when his heart races to one-six-five
You can see that fearfully remembered pain.

He has been dead four times and brought back to life
He is afraid the next time will be his last
And yet he just keeps going
Long walks his remedy
For battling his long-time enemy
Ventricular tachycardia.

He tells us about his flashy cars
When he was a king
Driving across America
Just doing his own thing.
He invested wisely and lived very well
Kept driving until he was seventy-five
His heart rate is one-six-two
And he is fast asleep.

He is really fighting old age
Instead of seeing it as his friend
Instead of loving his future
He just wants the change to end.

So, he takes on the world to be powerful
Wants to be seen and to be heard
Afraid that his silence makes him invisible
He shouts more loudly now.

And in the quiet of the midnight hour
When he has nothing else to fight
When the certainty of tomorrow becomes clear
When the remorseless energy of old age wins,
When the power of his body begins to die

When he knows his memory is gone
When his once golden face becomes ashen,
And the hair on his head snowy grey.
When the heart still races at one-six-two

And it's unclear what's causing it all
He blames it on the work he does, the kids,
The stress and the traffic jams
As opposed to his ageing frame.

The Submariner sat there observing it all
He was the youngest of the three
He had experienced a multitude of pain
And was worried about it no more
He asked the Chauffeur and the Taxi Driver
Why they were so afraid
They said of what tomorrow brings
Afraid that there was no certainty
No beginning or end.
The Chauffeur said the future reveals nothing to me.
You would think after seventy-six years
I would be able to see a lot more
But the older I get, the more uncertain it all seems
Between the memory fade and the energy jade
I have no idea what the next second will bring.

Out of the corner of my eye
A patient is gasping for air
He looks helpless and apologetic
As lack of oxygen makes him stare
The resus team rushes over
And resus him one more time

The man looks relieved, the resus team matter-of-factly disband
And we just carry on talking as before.

I said I was a Submariner, joined the Navy in sixty-five
Running away from a prearranged destiny
Created by everyone but me.
I did all the things I planned to do
Created a universe of my own
Thought I had everything under control

As if I could do it all alone
Now I have no answers to give
No certainty exists within me
No clarity of thought, just ideas I have bought
That cannot stand close scrutiny.

I have reached the Age of the Sage
I thought wisdom would have joined me by now
But all I have are sacks full of questions
And not one answer I can give.

Life

I first met him on the day he was born.
He was lying down … just having a rest
Gently…trying to focus on the dewy morn
His only means of survival … his mother's breast.

His mother looked on in wonderment
Afraid to touch this fragile gift
The child looked on in wonderment
Afraid to leave this rock-like gift.

Bonds that last for eternity
Instantaneously coming to being
First days going by like infinity
First, of many days' child will be seeing.

I looked at him again when he was two years old
So confident that he was in control
Running now…jumping now…talking…endlessly bold
Future just something that will unfold.

Bright eyes beaming…
Cheeks so gleaming…
Eyes just streaming endlessly.
Fine teeth showing…

No tears flowing…
His childhood growing relentlessly.

I glimpsed him fleetingly by a lake
I guessed he was no more than five
He looked at me as if there was a mistake
He knew for the first time that he was alive.

Thrusting now…demanding now
The world was his…and his alone
Fighting here…delighting there
Sitting on Daddy's shoulders…all the way home.

Bright eyes beaming…
Cheeks so gleaming…
Eyes just streaming endlessly.
Fine teeth showing…
No tears flowing…
His childhood growing relentlessly.

At sixteen, he was a handsome young man
Listening to nothing but his own voice
The meaning of life…the yin and the yang
Were too simple to ruffle his elegant poise.

I met him again at twenty-five
The first day of the rest of his life
Full of himself and a little naïve
Confidence brimming…sharp as a knife.

Contact lens beaming…
Hard cheeks gleaming…

Eyes just roving endlessly.
A capped tooth showing...
A few tears flowing...
His childhood dying relentlessly.

It was seven long years till I saw him again
Up to his eyeballs in nappies and pins
House rent and rate...baby irate...still numb from lifelong pains
His world just going into an infinite spin.

Money was now his God-like model
His strategy for survival...just a little askew
His hopes and dreams...in a warren-like muddle
No clear future...just a frightening view.

Spectacled eyes dreaming...
Sallow cheeks steaming...
Aches and pains hurting endlessly.
False teeth showing...
Grey hairs flowing...
His middle years dying relentlessly.
His children missing...
His lifestyle ending...
His heart just aching endlessly.
New clothes not coming...
Money...just going
Reality just hitting him relentlessly...
Reality...just hitting him relentlessly...
Reality...just hitting him...relentlessly.

And in the stillness of his solitude
When he thought he was alone

I heard him say to the wind.

"Why the pain...why the long road of sorrow...?

Is my life not worth any bends...?

Oh...! For a life of one sweet tomorrow...

Where loneliness isn't my only friend..."

Spectacled eyes not seeing...

Gristled cheeks convening...

Grandchildren growing endlessly.

False teeth not fitting...

The toupee no longer sitting...

Coming to terms reluctantly.

New friendships beginning,

Mind...no longer spinning...

Years going by relentlessly.

Stairs...getting higher...

Exertions...getting rarer...

Some good friends dying unexpectedly.

Armchair...so inviting...

Sleep is so exciting...

Seeing family more frequently.

He was looking in the mirror

In one of his eightieth years

When he recognised me

As what he was trying to find

We held each other...

And we shed a few tears

I...the long lost...

Forgotten friend...

Was his peace of mind.

Epilogue.
I was with him on the day that he died
He was lying down just having a rest
Desperately...trying to focus on life...as it's implied
And gently falling...back...into Mother Nature's breast.
In the end, he smiled and said he felt a little odd
Then finally gave himself to God.

The Black Man's Song

I want to tell you a story
I promise it won't take long
It's about a tribe filled with glory
It's called 'The Black Man's Song.'

We the people of the Promised Land,
Were stolen in our innocence,
Taken by an unmerciful hand,
And cut off from our inheritance.

We had our native culture,
We had our native tongue,
Suddenly there was a vulture,
Forcing us to sing his song.

He took us in his stinking ship,
Three hundred at a time,
Our incentive was his stinging whip,
Our food just gruel and lime.

For long, long months…imprisoned by the seas,
In the bottom of his pit.
No recreation…just his histories.
We tired, dying, in our own shit.

More than a half passed away on those rides.
Too sick, forgetting to be proud.
Bodies thrown to the ever-present tide.
While the wailing grew so loud.
While the wailing grew so loud.

They must always be remembered
They will not die in vain
Their bodies now dismembered
Must illuminate our brain

Finally, landed on that raucous beach
Tired, bedraggled, and chained
The road ahead, their imagination can't reach
So, a numbness their hearts maintained

The whip was the second thing they felt
The first was degrade and shame
At their master's feet, position knelt
Humiliation? Always the same

They worked for sixteen hours a day
And then they slept for five
Hard labour, their only pay
Their only thought, to stay alive

If Willie Lynch existed, he would have said,
"Slavery is a psychological game
Where the master makes the rules
Being afraid to die is just the same
For wise men or for fools."

In captivity, we paid the price
For lack of unity and trust
The master kept some of us feeling nice
On others, he gratified his lust

For three centuries, we helped the master
All his countries became great
Economically, they could not grow faster
The blacks just grew inanimate

In Jamaica, 'Mada Nanny and Cudjoe' fought and won
Very small victories
Tacky took over where they'd begun
Trying to brighten, our history

Left isolated up in the hills
The rebellion could not, and did not spread
The master sat there counting his kills
Got another boatload of 'niggers' to replace the dead
Our women took the brunt
Of the master's attack
They were not important
Even less, could they fight back?

Raped, vandalised, and scandalised
Self-respect and dignity drained
Through fear, they were totally hypnotised
And the master's will was maintained

Men seeding children for three hundred years
Painfully discharged from responsibility

Whipped, flogged, and killed, the scars they bear
To remind us of their sensitivity

We say that Uncle Toms were nought
Paradoxically, they saved our race
Outgunned, outmanoeuvred, and outthought
They kept us from our final resting place

All our heroes fought and died
Too proud to toe the line
Too impatient to wait for a turned tide
Survivors? No. Heroes? Fine

Peer into the master's mind
And if you try to understand
Greed and ignorance, you'll find
He's a savage, he is not a man

Some African chiefs…also to blame
For this history of my race
They chose baubles, trinkets and fame
To them, I give no solace
Slowly, the tide began to turn
Toussaint L'Ouverture beat the French
Slavery economics was now being spurned
The Europeans couldn't take the stench

Salvation came in thirty-three
And Christianity moved in
The blacks thought they were now free
Deftly, Christianity moved in

In 1838, we thought we'd come to the end of the war
But it was only an interlude
They gave us our freedom…then charged us a star
Just for water and for food

America took a war and thirty more years
To do what Europe did in 'peace'
America's South, shed a lot of tears
When blacks they could no longer fleece

The Ku Klux Klan was now in charge
Of the white man's vanity
They maimed, they hung, and they barraged
Our people, with their insanity

In the North, token 'niggers' were everywhere
Even in great seats of power

The master's conscience pricked for twenty years
In the span of man's history…less than an hour
The light-skinned of our race now took the lead
Becoming worse than the white
Ridiculed the dark…ignored our needs
And made the white, feel right

We were in the wilderness another twenty years
While the First World waged its war
We heard our 'blues' through musical ears
Some of us through feather and tar

We made up our songs in our own way
Only we knew what we were going through

The hardship, the fear, the lack of pay
Were what made us sing so 'Blue'

In Africa...the people were waking
Up to what Europe had done
Haile Selassie sent Italy quaking
Back to the Mediterranean
Africa started to take stock
Of the remains of our diamonds and gold
But they were in for a real shock
All they were left were VD and cold

A political force we had to find
And Marcus Garvey came to the fore
He made and gave us the Black Star Line
But the black man needed more

We meandered about for twenty more years
Like a company without a boss
Inferiority complexes, and all the other fears
Meant we weren't worth a toss

Then nature sent us Martin Luther King
Like a black knight, he did strut
He said if we wanted to change anything
We had to get off our butt

His voice was a voice with a mission
His words were transparently clear
He allowed us to see a vision
Of a black man with pride and no fear

If you have ever heard his speeches,
If you have ever seen the man talk
In everything he says he beseeches
That we've got to find the spark

The spark to ignite the fire
Of black unity and pride
That will take us on the higher
Plain, where we must ride

I'll never forget the day they killed him
I'm sure the world did pause
I'm sure the sun did go a little dim
He was fighting for a higher cause

We were lucky in the seventies
Marley came after MLK
Although only in his twenties
He sure had a lot to say

He reinforced what MLK had said
He did it with a musical beat
On stage when he was whiplashing his dread
He sure looked a musical treat

Marvin Gaye said the good die young
And he is gone as well
I wonder why the good die young
Because they had so much to tell?

So, let's look at twenty oh one five
See how far we've got

Well, at least we're still alive
Though, some wish we were not

In Africa, our people are still dying
While richer blacks look on
In South America, our people are crying
While powerful blacks look on

In the Caribbean, the place of my birth
America is still in control
The politicians, for all they are worth
Are too afraid to even be bold

In England, the prisons are filled
With the sperm of our future tribes
In asylums, our brains are grilled
Because we cannot accept their vibes

In the street, we now riot and loot
Because we've not been employed
In our veins, we're beginning to shoot
Oblivion, that's all we've got, to be enjoyed.

And Maya Angelou cries
And still, we rise
And my heart, my soul, my spirit replies
My father is the Great God OSIRIS
And I lived in the delta of the Nile
We were sent here to learn peace and forgiveness
And these lessons are taking a while
So…we take our pain and go forward

New horizons are ahead,
They're not too far
Keep remembering our past,
Remember every word
Let's never ever forget…
Exactly who we are.

Stay Focussed

Remember to:
Stay focused in the middle of the noise and bustle
And remember the peace and tranquillity of silence.
While you are strong, sometimes being
Seen as weak and fragile is the best line to take.
You don't have to wait until you are loved before you love.

Speak your truth quietly and clearly.
But listen, listen to all information
For sometimes, the wisest words,
Are spoken by the biggest fools
And everyone has an important story to tell.

Walk away from the rudeness of aggressive people
Once you have heard what they have to say
Staying and returning their aggression…
Makes you worse than they,
For you know better.

Do not compare yourself with anyone else,
For this will either make you vain or bitter.
For always there will be greater and,
Lesser achievements than yours…

Take pride in what you do,
And what you achieve.

Remember...
Dreams are reality awaiting their time
Stay focused on your dreams.
For they are tomorrow's reality
Pursue your career,
It is an important part of the baton
In the relay race of life

Trust everyone until they prove...
They cannot be trusted.
This may be painful now and then.
But in the long run of time,
You will find that people,
Are virtuous, caring, loving.
Protective, heroic, giving,
And trustworthy.

Be yourself.
Evolve and grow.
Mature like wine.
But do not change
See the world, understand its strengths and weaknesses
But maintain and love your own sense of self at all times.

Listen well to the words of the wise.
You will find that the years of life,
Seeing and observing, have made the elders,
Arrive closer to the fundamental truths.

Some of them may appear as if they will not know,
But listen, before dismissing them as fakes.
They may surprise you.

Keep your mind, your body, and your soul,
Clean, healthy, and as pure as life will allow.
But do not become obsessed with this.
Remember...the ultimate enjoyment in life,
Is when it all balances.

Do not seek loneliness for a friend
But do not run away from the medicinal qualities,
Of solitude.
Be gentle with yourself
In a disciplined way
Forgetting not that you,
Are a child of the universe
No greater than the atom
No less than the stars
You were destined to be here
Time and space are unfolding
Exactly as it is meant to do.

Be in harmony with your god...
Be it Nature or Jehovah,
Whatever you decide it to be.
And remember,
In the confusion of pursuing your dreams,
Be at peace with yourself.
For with all its politics,

Pain, lies, deceit, wrongs…
And broken dreams,
It is still a beautiful world.

Stay Focussed.

About the Author

Roy Merchant was born in Jamaica. He left there in 1961 to join his parents in England. He enlisted in the Royal Navy in 1965 and became a submariner, spending most of his submarine years in Singapore, Hong Kong and other parts of the Far East.

Having left the Navy in 1970, he retrained as an Electronics Engineer, then Technical Manager in a large television rental company in the 1970s.

In the mid-'80s, he moved into local government as a senior manager in a London local authority. Retiring in 2014, Roy took a new path and started a Health and well-being company catering mainly for the African Caribbean community while dedicating more time to writing and performing poetry across London.

This book is his fifth. His fourth is a collection of short stories called *Images*, his third a novella called *Distorted Lens*, his second is *20 Things I Wish I Knew At 20*, and his first is entitled *Walking In The Shadows Of Death*.

Published by:

Relentless Realities
Roy Merchant   Writer and Performance Poet
Website: https://www.relentless-realities.com
Email: roy@relentless-realities.com